America's Leaders

The *Secretary of the* INTERIOR

by Kate Davis

BLACKBIRCH
PRESS

THOMSON
★
GALE

San Diego • Detroit • New York • San Francisco • Cleveland • New Haven, Conn. • Waterville, Maine • London • Munich

© 2002 by Blackbirch Press™. Blackbirch Press™ is an imprint of The Gale Group, Inc., a division of Thomson Learning, Inc.

Blackbirch Press™ and Thomson Learning™ are trademarks used herein under license.

For more information, contact
The Gale Group, Inc.
27500 Drake Rd.
Farmington Hills, MI 48331-3535
Or you can visit our Internet site at http://www.gale.com

ALL RIGHTS RESERVED
No part of this work covered by the copyright hereon may be reproduced or used in any form or by any means—graphic, electronic, or mechanical, including photocopying, recording, taping, Web distribution or information storage retrieval systems—without the written permission of the publisher.

Every effort has been made to trace the owners of copyrighted material.

Photo credits: cover background, back cover, pages 3, 4, 5, 6, 8, 9, 10, 1, 12, 15, 16, 19, 20, 24, 26-27, 28-29, 30-31, 32 © Creatas; Udall cover inset, Norton cover inset, pages 4, 9, 11, 12, 13, 15, 16, 17, 18, 19, 20, 21, 23, 25, 26, 27 © CORBIS; cover background inset, pages 8, 14, 22, 27, 28, 29, 30, 31 © PhotoDisc; page 5 © Dover Publications; page 6, 7 © Federal Emergency Management Association

LIBRARY OF CONGRESS CATALOGING-IN-PUBLICATION DATA

Davis, Kate.
 The Secretary of the Interior / by Kate Davis.
  p. cm. — (America's leaders series)
Includes index.
Summary: An introduction to the Cabinet-level post of Secretary of the Interior, discussing the selection of the Secretary, duties, organizational structure, as well as a sample day's responsibilities.
 ISBN 1-56711-664-7
 1. United States. Dept. of the Interior. Office of the Secretary—Juvenile literature. [1. United States. Dept. of the Interior. Office of the Secretary.] I. Title. II. Series.
 JK868 .D38 2003
 333.7'0973—dc21   2002003950

Printed in United States
10 9 8 7 6 5 4 3 2 1

Table of Contents

Caring for the Country 4

The Secretary's Responsibilities 6

Who Works with the Secretary? 10

Where Does the Secretary Work? 12

Requirements for Secretary 16

A Time of Crisis 20

A Secretary's Day 24

Fascinating Facts 26

Glossary 28

For More Information .30

Index 32

Caring for the Country

More than 200 years ago, a group of men wrote a document, the U.S. Constitution, which established the American government. The authors of the Constitution divided the government into 3 separate branches with equal powers. The legislative branch was made up of the Senate and the House of Representatives. The judicial branch was the nation's court system, with the Supreme Court as the highest court. The third branch of government was the executive branch, which was led by the president.

Ever since George Washington, the first president, took office, presidents have needed people to help them operate the executive branch. In 1789, the U.S. Congress voted to establish departments in the executive branch to assist the president. The leader of each department was called a

Secretary of the Interior Gale Norton walks past a redwood tree in a national park in California.

secretary. Together, the secretaries formed a group known as the president's cabinet.

The Department of the Interior was not one of the original cabinet departments. By the middle of the 1800s, however, the United States had acquired millions of square miles of new land. The land and its resources needed to be managed.

> **USA FACT**
> In 2002, the secretary's yearly salary was $161,200.

In 1849, on his last day in office, President James Polk signed an act of Congress creating the Department of the Interior. The next president, Zachary Taylor, appointed the first secretary of the interior, Thomas Ewing.

Since then, 47 men and one woman have served as secretary of the interior. The first woman to hold the position was Gale Norton. She became secretary under President George W. Bush in 2001.

In 1849, Thomas Ewing became the first secretary of the interior.

The Secretary's Responsibilities

More than one-fifth of the land in the United States is owned by the federal government. This land is under the control of the Department of the Interior. The secretary is responsible for managing more than 440 million acres of federal land. That includes 360 national parks and more than 500 wildlife refuges. His or her main job is to make decisions about the land, water, minerals, and wildlife of the United States. A secretary might decide when to send in firefighters to combat fire

The secretary of the interior develops plans for fighting fires in national forests.

The secretary of the interior is responsible for managing national parks, such as Everglades National Park in Florida.

in a national forest or how to get cleanup crews to handle a large oil spill. She might order a dam to be removed to restore the natural flow of a river. She may order a study of the impact of drilling for oil in a natural habitat. A secretary can decide whether to allow snowmobiles in a national park or whether to place an animal on the endangered species list.

The secretary is also responsible for America's many historic places, which include famous battlefields and historic homes. She or he decides how a famous place should be preserved and sets aside money to repair, rebuild, or restore it. The secretary can prevent other historic areas from being destroyed or changed by real-estate development.

The secretary sets aside federal funds to keep national parks such as Yellowstone ready to welcome visitors.

The secretary is responsible for the interests and education of Native Americans.

The secretary is also responsible for the well-being of Native Americans and their lands. When oil, gas, or timber is taken from Native American lands, or when the land is rented for use by ranchers, the secretary is responsible for making certain that the money earned from those activities is paid to Native Americans.

USA Fact

In 1994, lawyers representing about 300,000 Native Americans filed a lawsuit against the Department of the Interior. The suit claimed that for more than a century, money owed to Native Americans for mining, grazing, and logging their land was lost, stolen, or never collected. The lawyers claim the government owes the Native Americans more than $10 billion.

Who Works with the Secretary?

The secretary of the interior needs help to manage a department that oversees millions of acres of land and water. To manage the department, he or she meets with a staff regularly. These meetings include a chief of staff, deputy chief of staff, deputy secretary of the interior, and associate deputy secretary. A secretary also needs people to ask for information about specific questions or issues. These people include a science adviser, adviser for Indian affairs, and an adviser for Alaska affairs.

The Department of the Interior has more than 70,000 employees and more than 200,000 volunteer workers.

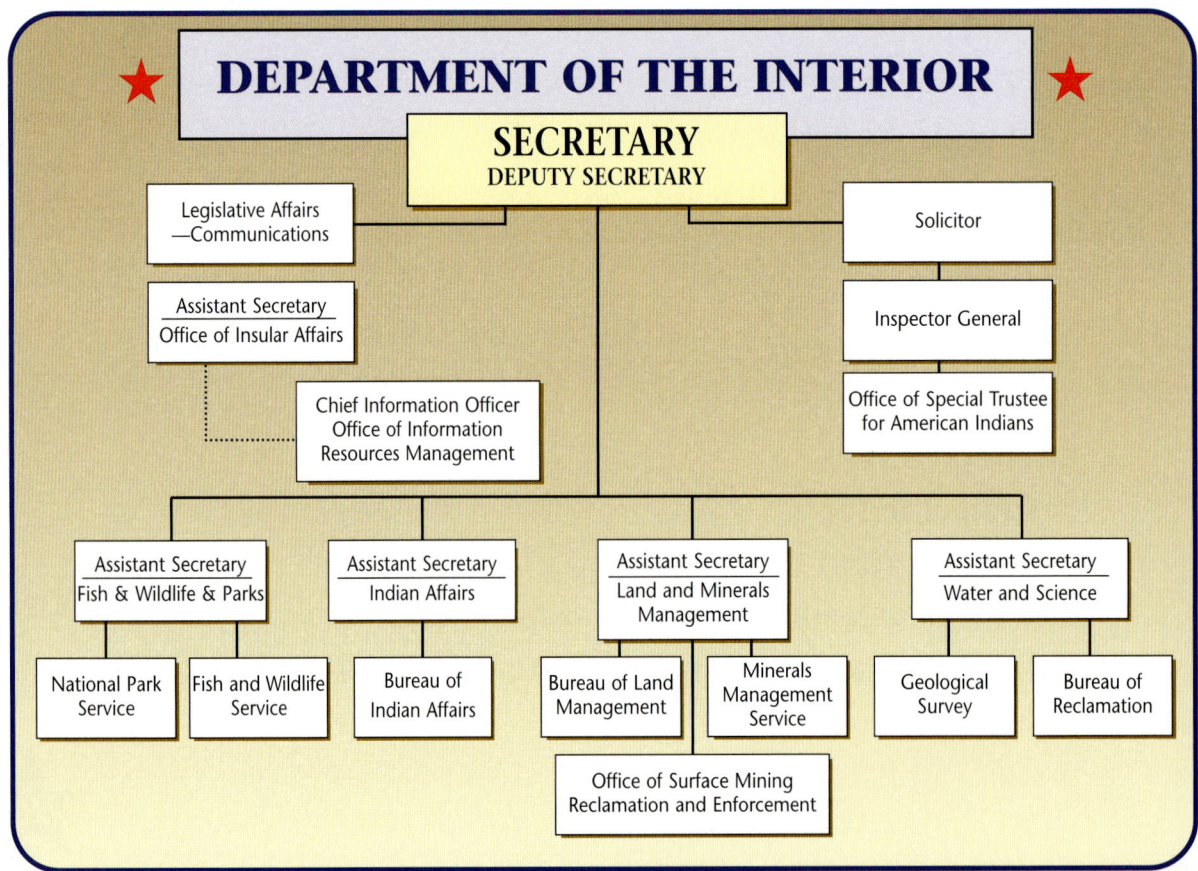

Stewart Udall (third from right) was the secretary of the interior in the cabinet of President Lyndon B. Johnson.

The secretary also meets regularly with staff members who communicate the department's decisions and policies to the public and to other branches of government.

In addition to the people who work daily with the secretary, there are also heads of bureaus and offices within the department. These people include the director of the national park service, deputy commissioner for Indian affairs, and the assistant secretary of land and minerals management.

> **USA Fact**
>
> The main divisions of the department are the Bureau of Land Management, Fish and Wildlife Service, National Park Service, Bureau of Indian Affairs, Minerals Management Service, Office of Surface Mining, and the Office of Insular Affairs (formerly called the Office of Territories). An Office of Water and Science includes the U.S. Geological Survey and the Bureau of Reclamation.

Where Does the Secretary Work?

The Department of the Interior Building is located in Washington, D.C. It is one of the largest government office buildings in the nation's capital. This granite and limestone structure takes up an entire city block on C Street, one block west of the White House. Much of the Interior Building is lined with marble. The building also has a public museum and a collection of paintings, murals, and sculptures.

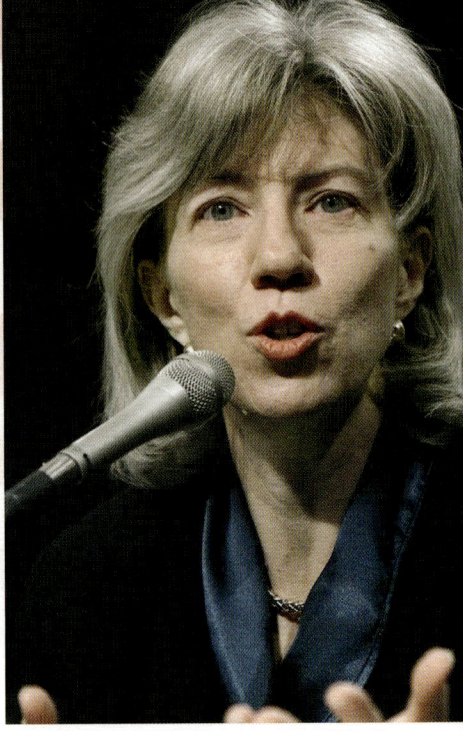

Secretary Gale Norton testified before the Senate Energy and Natural Resources Committee in 2001.

The White House

Once a week, the secretary of the interior meets with the president and other cabinet members in the Cabinet Room, next to the Oval Office in the West Wing of the White House. There, overlooking the Rose Garden, the department officers discuss national or foreign problems.

USA Fact

The Department of the Interior manages mineral development in more than 1.4 billion acres of ocean floor. This area, called the continental shelf, extends for about 200 miles from all coastal areas of the United States. Some areas of the continental shelf have been developed for oil drilling.

On Capitol Hill

The secretary also appears before committees in the Senate and the House of Representatives. The secretary appears before the budget committee in the House to answer questions about the way the department spends about $10 billion each year.

In the Senate, the secretary may appear before the Environment and Public Works Committee and the Indian Affairs Committee. Federal lands produce more than one-third of the coal and one-fourth of the oil used in the United States each year. The secretary may appear before senators to explain the ways that the environment is affected by mining and drilling. The department is also responsible for the education of more than

The secretary must protect the environment in areas of federal land where coal and other resources are mined.

50,000 Native American children. It also manages land on which the Native Americans live. This responsibility also requires the secretary to appear before Senate committees to explain any actions of the department.

On the Road

The secretary does not work only in Washington. He or she often makes speeches at department-related events around the country. Such an event may be the opening of a national park, a hydroelectric dam, or a renovated historic site. The secretary may also speak to groups that are concerned about protecting the environment.

Historic parks, such as this Civil War battlefield in Tennessee, are under the care of the Department of the Interior.

Secretary Bruce Babbitt speaks at the opening of a national park in California that was previously a military base.

If natural disasters, such as forest fires, floods, or oil spills, involve federal lands, the secretary gets involved. She may go to the affected area to make decisions to send in government personnel to assist the damage-control or cleanup effort. The secretary may also personally inspect areas operated by the department, such as mines, forests, and seashores.

USA Fact

The secretary of the interior oversees the Bureau of Indian Affairs, which has responsibility for 560 federally recognized Native American and Alaskan tribes.

Requirements for Secretary

The Constitution does not give specific requirements for holding an office in the president's cabinet. In many cases, a president nominates a secretary of the interior who shares his views about important environmental issues. In the last decades of the 20th century, the

Americans who believe in Wise Use feel that federal land should be used for logging.

People opposed to Wise Use generally belong to environmental groups.

appointment of the secretary of the interior became controversial. Americans disagree over environmental laws, energy development, and land use.

Disagreements arose mainly over the use of federal land. In the 1970s, a movement known as "Wise Use" was organized. This was meant to defeat what some people saw as environmental laws being too strict. A Wise Use document stated that "access to public land should be unrestricted for logging, mining, drilling, motorized recreation, and all commercial enterprise."

People who took the opposing viewpoint generally belonged to environmentalist groups. These people opposed any commercial use of public land. Many felt that the environmental laws were not strong enough, and that those already passed were not well enforced.

Oil drilling along national seashores is a topic of debate among Wise Use advocates and environmental groups.

In the early 21st century, oil drilling in the Alaska National Wildlife Refuge became a disputed topic. Wise Use advocates and environmentalists disagreed strongly. Some people felt that the nation's energy needs made it necessary to drill in the wildlife refuge. Others felt that the damage to the environment from drilling would be too severe. In 2001, President George W. Bush nominated Gale Norton as the secretary of the interior. Norton shared Bush's opinion that the oil drilling should be allowed in the Alaska National Wildlife Refuge.

> **USA FACT**
> If a president dies, the secretary of the interior is eighth in line to take over the presidency, after the vice president, legislators, and other cabinet members.

Norton, like all nominees for cabinet positions, had to undergo an FBI background check of her personal, medical, financial, and legal history. All nominees for secretary must appear in hearings before a Senate committee. Often these hearings involve sharp political disagreements between lawmakers who support strong environmental laws and those who believe in principles of Wise Use. After the nominee appears before the Senate committee, the full Senate votes to confirm or deny him or her.

Swearing In

Once he or she is approved, the secretary is sworn in. The ceremony may be a large formal affair in the Interior Building's auditorium. The president, the chief justice of the Supreme Court, speakers, and congressional members will often attend. The secretary usually makes a brief speech that explains his or her goals for the department.

Secretary Gale Norton is sworn in before a Senate hearing in 2001.

A Time of Crisis

Less than 2 months after Interior Secretary Manuel Lujan took office in 1989, he faced one of the worst environmental disasters in U.S. history. An oil tanker ran aground off the coast of Alaska, and spilled 11 million gallons of oil into Prince William Sound. It was the largest oil spill ever within U.S. borders.

Just after midnight on March 24, the tanker, *Exxon Valdez*, left the Port of Valdez with a full load of crude oil from the Alaskan pipeline. Captain Joseph Hazelwood had been drinking and was also extemely tired. As the ship made its way out of port, its hull struck Bligh Reef and burst open. Oil gushed into the sound. Within days, more than 700 miles of coastline were coated with tarry balls of oil. Eventually, the oil coated almost 1,500 miles of shoreline.

Manuel Lujan appeared before Congress to support stronger environmental laws after the Exxon Valdez oil spill.

The spill killed hundreds of thousands of shore birds. As many as 5,500 sea otters died. Harbor seals, porpoises, stellar sea lions, and beluga and killer whales were also killed. The oil had a devastating effect on the fishing industry. Mussel beds and fish hatcheries were polluted. People in the region's fishing villages had their livelihood damaged.

Oil-soaked seaweed is pulled from the water of Prince William Sound after the Exxon Valdez *created the largest oil spill within U.S. borders.*

Lujan immediately sent people to work with Alaskan response teams and federal agencies to clean up the area. Marine experts from the Fish and Wildlife Service, along with many volunteers, tried to save the region's sea birds and mammals. Unfortunately, bad weather and lack of proper equipment made the effort extra difficult.

State and federal governments sued the Exxon company for $1 billion. Exxon paid $100 million in fines and $900 million for recovery. Lujan said, "This

Thousands of shore birds were killed by the oil spill.

settlement serves notice to all that carelessness in transporting oil can have costly consequences."

In 1990, Congress passed the Oil Pollution Act, which required stricter rules for oil tankers, owners, and operators. A council was set up, with members of the Department of the Interior, to oversee recovery of the environment. Some environmentalists predicted that it would take 80 years to restore seabird populations.

Another Time of Crisis

The secretary of the interior who served the longest was Harold Ickes. He held the post under President Franklin Roosevelt from 1933 until 1945. Like Roosevelt, Ickes took office during the years when the United States was suffering under the Great Depression. More than one-fourth of the American workforce was unemployed, and millions of Americans lived on the verge of poverty and starvation.

When Roosevelt took office, he established a number of programs to put government money back into the economy. Ickes was given more than $3 billion and put in charge of a federal program called the Public Works

Harold Ickes was secretary during the Great Depression.

Administration (PWA). Ickes slowly began to hand out the money to fund various public improvement projects across the country. The PWA put millions to work and led to the construction of some of the best-known sites in the United States.

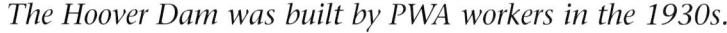

The greatest works of the PWA include the Hoover Dam, the Bonneville Dam, the University of Utah Library, the St. Louis Municipal Auditorium, the Oregon State Capitol, and the Lincoln Tunnel. PWA workers also constructed the Department of the Interior Building in Washington, D.C. PWA funds also paid for the construction of bridges, hospitals, ferry boats, post offices, and sewage disposal plants. Many PWA projects, such as the Hoover and Bonneville Dams, are still managed by the Department of the Interior today.

The Hoover Dam was built by PWA workers in the 1930s.

A Secretary's Day

The secretary's busy schedule means he or she must oversee tasks as varied as reintroducing wolves into national parks or making a presentation about drilling for oil in a wildlife refuge. Here is what a day might be like for the secretary of the interior.

6:00 AM	Wake, shower, dress; read newspaper response to speech on "the new environmentalism of Wise Use"
7:00 AM	Commute from home to Interior Building
7:30 AM	Interview candidate for head of new task force in Mineral Management Office
8:00 AM	Review preliminary budget figures from individual departments
9:00 AM	Meet with director of National Park Service to approve 15 new sites designated as National Historic Landmarks
9:30 AM	Receive agenda and files for weekly cabinet meeting
10:00 AM	Ride to White House; meet in Cabinet Room with president, senior staff, and department secretaries
12:15 PM	Review remarks with press secretary for address to National Press Club

Secretary Donald Hodel meets with firefighters who have fought blazes in national forests.

- **12:45 PM** Meet with firefighters to award medals for outstanding service
- **3:00 PM** Review latest court rulings concerning the suit over Indian Trust Management
- **4:30 PM** Meet with commissioner of Bureau of Reclamation and area farmers to discuss water supply from Klamath Basin Project in Oregon
- **6:30 PM** Change for evening engagement
- **7:00 PM** Attend opening reception at Interior Museum for new exhibition, "Land America Leaves Wild"
- **10:30 PM** Return home. Read president's directives on Native American schools
- **11:00 PM** Bed

Fascinating Facts

Thomas Ewing, the first secretary of the interior, was the father-in-law of William T. Sherman, the well-known Union general in the Civil War.

In the 1860s, **Secretary James Harlan** fired a poet who worked as a clerk at the Department of the Interior because he did not like a book the man had written. The poet was Walt Whitman, and the book was *Leaves of Grass*, a poetry collection that became a classic of American literature.

The Department of the Interior was originally in charge of the census and the patent offices. Those responsibilities were transferred to the Department of Commerce in 1903.

One of the most respected secretaries was **Stewart B. Udall** from Utah. He helped enact 4 major conservation laws, and won a lifetime achievement award for his environmental efforts.

Stewart Udall with First Lady Lady Bird Johnson.

Albert Fall is arrested by federal agents.

Secretary of the Interior **Albert B. Fall**, who served under President Warren G. Harding, was convicted and imprisoned for bribery in the Teapot Dome oilfield lease scandal of 1929.

President James A. Garfield's son, **James R. Garfield**, served as secretary of the interior in 1907 under Theodore Roosevelt.

The Department of the Interior manages one-fifth of all U.S. land.

The department's Bureau of Land Management, which controls mining operations of federal land, oversees more than twice as many acres underneath the surface of the earth than on it.

The Bureau of Reclamation manages 69,400 miles of canals. If all those canals flowed end to end, they would circle the earth almost 3 times.

Nine out of 10 employees of the Department of the Interior work at field offices throughout the country.

The secretary of the interior is responsible for managing national parks such as Zion National Park in Utah.

Glossary

administer—to manage or direct the workings of, or to have charge of

cabinet—a council of presidential advisers who help manage the government

Constitution—the document that established the U.S. government and that contains the principles and laws of the nation

continental shelf—the part of a continent that extends 200 miles out from a coastline

economy—the management of resources and earnings of a group or country

environment—the natural surroundings, including the air, water, minerals, and organisms

Bryce Canyon in Utah is a popular national park.

Coral reefs in Florida are under the protection of the Department of the Interior.

habitats—natural places for the life and growth of a plant or animal

hearings—formal sessions in which questions and answers are presented

Indian trust lands—Native American lands off of the reservation that are placed into trust, or agreement, with the federal government

reclamation—the act or process of reclaiming or restoring

regulations—rules and laws

resources—the supply and products of the land and water (such as coal, timber, and fish) and the value contained in them

wildlife refuge—land set aside for protection of fish and wildlife

For More Information

Publications

Office of Federal Register, National Archives and Records Administration. *United States Government Manual, 2000–2001.* Washington, DC: Government Printing Office, 2000

Peterson, David. *National Parks.* Danbury, CT: Children's Press, 2000.

Quiri, Patricia Ryan. *The Constitution.* Danbury, CT: Children's Press, 1999.

Wellman, Sam. *The Cabinet.* Broomall, PA: Chelsea House, 2001.

Web sites

Bureau of Land Management's Kid's Corner

"Walk on the Wild Side: Explore Your Public Lands"

http://www.blm.gov/education/00_kids/contents.html

Interesting information with activities for kids. Users can download a fun booklet.

National Park Service "Park Net"

http://www.nps.gov

The homepage for information on all the national parks and historic sites. Includes Visit Your Parks, Links to the Past, Nature Net, Park Smart, Info Zone, contests, etc.

U.S. Department of the Interior

http://www.doi.gov

Homepage with links to information about the secretary and transcripts of speeches; undergoing major revision in 2002.

U.S. Geologic Survey "Learning Web"

http://ask.usgs.gov/education.html

Tons of information for kids on exploring maps, science challenges, "TerraWeb," rock collecting, and much more. Lots of good links.

Index

adviser for Alaska affairs 11
adviser for Indian affairs 11
Alaska National Wildlife Refuge 18
Alaskan pipeline 20
Bligh Reef 20
Bonneville Dam 23
Bureau of Land Management 27
Bureau of Reclamation 27
Bush, George W. 5, 18
cabinet 5, 12, 16, 19, 24
chief justice of the Supreme Court 19
chief of staff 10
Civil War 26
Congress 4, 22
Constitution 4, 16
Department of Commerce . . . 26
Department of the Interior 5, 6, 13, 14, 22, 23, 26, 27
Department of the Interior Building 12, 19, 23, 24
deputy chief of staff 10
deputy commissioner for Indian affairs 11
deputy secretary of the interior 10
director of the national park service 11

Environment and Public Works Committee 13
environmentalists 17, 18, 19, 22, 24
Ewing, Thomas 5, 26
Exxon 21
Exxon Valdez 20
Fall, Albert B. 27
FBI 19
Fish and Wildlife Service 21
Garfield, James A. 27
Garfield, James R. 27
government branches
 executive 4
 judicial 4
 legislative 4
Great Depression 22
Harding, Warren G. 27
Harlan, James 26
Hazelwood, Joseph 20
Hoover Dam 23
House of Representatives . . 4, 13
Ickes, Harold 22
Indian Affairs Committee 13
Lincoln Tunnel 23
Lujan, Manuel 20-21
national parks 6, 7, 14, 24
Native Americans 9, 14
Norton, Gale 5, 18

Oil Pollution Act 22
Oregon State Capitol 23
Oval Office 2
Polk, James 5
president 4, 12, 16, 19, 24
Prince William Sound 20
Public Works Administration . . . 23
Roosevelt, Franklin 22
Roosevelt, Theodore 27
science adviser 11
secretary of the interior
 advisers 10-11
 becoming secretary 16-17
 responsibilities . . 5, 6-9, 12, 13, 14, 15, 20, 21, 22, 23, 24-25
 workplace 12-15
Senate 4, 13, 14, 19
Sherman, William T. 26
St. Louis Municipal Auditorium 23
Supreme Court 4
Taylor, Zachary 5
Teapot Dome scandal 27
Udall, Stewart B. 26
University of Utah Library 23
Washington, D.C. 12, 14
White House 12, 24
Wise Use movement 17, 18, 19, 24